He Was Clever

───●───

A folk tale from Russia

Written by Tony Bradman and Tom Bradman

Illustrated by Juanbjuan Oliver

Collins

2

One day, the king came across an old book in the darkest corner of the palace library. He quickly realised the book was magical and that it would help him to play his greatest trick of all. He thought for a while, worked out a cunning plan and hugged himself with glee. Then he sent a servant to summon his daughter.

Her name was Olga, and she was sweet and kind, and as beautiful as a sunny summer morning. She was clever as well, but unlike her father, she wasn't bothered whether anybody knew that. So she kept her cleverness to herself, and was perfectly happy. Or at least she was until the king revealed what he had in mind.

"I've sent a message out to all the young men in the land, Olga," he said, with a smile. "I'll give you as a wife to the first one who can pass a special test."

"Oh, Father!" said Olga, horrified. "I don't want to be anybody's wife!"

"Relax, my dear," said the king, his smile growing even wider. "It's going to be a very hard test. In fact, nobody's going to pass it, not in a million years."

Olga hoped he was right. But she was worried all the same …

5

⇥ Chapter 2 ⇤

The king was a little disappointed when only three young men turned up at the palace a few days later. It seemed his reputation for being a trickster had put everybody else off. Still, it was the quality of the trick that counted, he thought, and not the number of people he managed to fool. So he welcomed them anyway.

They were all princes, and their names were Misha,
Sasha and Pavel. They sat at the great table in
the dining hall, eating the feast the king had provided.
Olga was there too, and shyly studied them.
Prince Misha and Prince Sasha were both tall and
good-looking, but Olga decided pretty quickly that they
were extremely dull.

Prince Pavel was not quite so tall or so good-looking.
But there was definitely something about him that Olga
rather liked, and he seemed to like her too. Prince Misha
and Prince Sasha talked to her father throughout
the meal, ignoring her. Prince Pavel, however, kept his
eyes on her, and the minutes flew past as they talked.

"Right, it's time I told you lads about the test," said
the king eventually. "All you have to do is hide – and
the winner will be the one that I can't find."

"Is that it?" said Prince Misha. "I thought it would be much tougher!"

"Me too," said Prince Sasha. "It hardly seems worth bothering – "

"Of course it is!" Pavel said angrily. "I'd do anything to win the hand of Princess Olga. You should be grateful that this test will be so easy."

Princess Olga blushed and gave him a lovely smile. The king, however, just smirked.

Chapter 3

Prince Misha and Prince Sasha tossed a coin to see who'd go first, completely ignoring Prince Pavel. Olga thought that was unfair and wanted to say something, but it was too late.

Prince Misha called out "Heads!" and that's how the coin fell. "Excellent!" he said. "Perhaps I should've told you, I've always been absolutely brilliant at playing hide-and-seek. Especially the hiding part." He laughed and ran out of the dining hall.

Olga turned to her father, who was just standing there. "Aren't you supposed to be counting to ten?" she said.

The king shrugged and smiled. "I could count to a million and it wouldn't make any difference," he said. "I'll find him no matter where he tries to hide." This was true – even though the palace was enormous, with hundreds of rooms and cellars and attics and cupboards and cubbyholes and nooks and crannies.

Prince Misha chose a hiding place as far away from
the dining hall as possible, in a dark room that had
almost been forgotten. But the king found him without
any trouble at all. Everyone was amazed, of course,
which was exactly what the king wanted.

"Ah well, first the worst, second the best," laughed
Prince Sasha. "I won't make it so easy for you, your
majesty – I'm pretty good at hide-and-seek myself!"
Then he ran out of the dining hall.

He'd already decided to hide outside, in the palace grounds. They were enormous too, with barracks and stables and gardens and greenhouses, and even a forest.

Prince Sasha chose a hiding place under a tangled bush as far from the palace as possible. But the king found him just as quickly.

"Incredible!" said Prince Misha and Prince Sasha. "How did you do it?"

Olga thought she'd like to know that as well.

❧ Chapter 4 ❧

Prince Misha and Prince Sasha were bad losers, and soon departed. The king saw them off at the gate, leaving Olga alone with Prince Pavel for a moment.

"I've something to confess," said Olga, shyly, blushing once more. "I'd like you to pass the test. So I'll help you to find the best hiding place."

"That's wonderful!" said Prince Pavel, his eyes shining. "But don't worry – I've a special, well … ability that means your father won't be able to find me."

"Really?" said Olga, rather surprised. "What exactly is this … ability?"

Prince Pavel looked round to make sure nobody could hear him. "I can change my shape," he whispered. "I can become any animal or object I want to."

Olga frowned: how could it be true? She thought that
perhaps he was trying to impress her – she knew boys
sometimes did that sort of thing, especially princes.
She wanted to tell him he didn't have to, but suddenly
her father came back.

18

"And then there was one!" said the king, laughing.
"Off you go and hide, Prince Pavel. It won't be for long,
though – I promise I'll find you just as quickly."

Prince Pavel headed for the door, but Olga held
him back. She was sure now that her father was
doing something very cunning, and she needed time
to investigate. And because she was his daughter and
clever, she knew how to handle him.

"Hold on a second, Father," she said. "You should give him three chances. That way, we'll get three more opportunities to see how brilliantly clever you are."

"I like it!" said the king. "Three chances it is. I'll even count this time."

He covered his face with his hands and started counting.

Prince Pavel smiled at Olga; then – to her astonishment – he turned himself into a cat and ran out.

But the king still found him just as quickly as the others.

⤙ Chapter 5 ⤚

Olga had watched it happen, yet she still couldn't believe it. Prince Pavel had padded round the palace for a while, then settled down on an armchair and curled up, pretending to be fast asleep. Olga had thought that it was a brilliant disguise. Lots of cats lived in the palace, and her father could never tell one from another.

It had taken the king a little longer to find Prince Pavel,
but not much. He'd counted to ten; then set off in search
of the prince, stopping for a few moments in his study.
He'd emerged and quickly found the right armchair,
almost as if he'd been told where to look. Then Prince
Pavel had changed back to his normal form.

"Not bad, my boy," the king said, smugly. "You certainly did better than the other two. But I'm far too clever to be fooled by anyone, even someone who can change their shape."

"It's not over yet," said Prince Pavel. He'd been shocked when his own trick hadn't worked, but he'd soon recovered. "I have two more chances."

"Of course you do!" said the king, grinning. "So let's get on with it – " He covered his face and began counting again, and Prince Pavel looked at Olga.

She took his hand and squeezed it. "I know you can do it, Pavel!" she said.

Prince Pavel smiled and kissed her cheek. Then he turned into a cat once more, and ran out of the palace.

He changed shape several times – he turned into a dog, then a magpie – and Olga could see that he was trying to find the best disguise. At last he made his mind up. He turned into a tiny ant and hid in a hole in the ground.

Olga was sure her father couldn't possibly find him. But she was wrong.

The king slowly counted to ten, then set off at last in search of Prince Pavel, only stopping for a few moments in his study. He soon went out of the palace – and quickly found the hole in the ground where a certain tiny ant was hiding. Olga's heart sank. Now they only had one chance left.

Chapter 6

"What a shame this is your last attempt," said the king. "I've very much enjoyed our game!"

"Why hurry things, Father?" asked Olga, starting to get an idea. "Pavel's tired. You want him at his best when you beat him one final time, don't you?"

"Hmmm, perhaps you're right," mused the king, stroking his chin. "Everyone will be much more impressed when I find you if you're fresh and rested. Good thinking, my girl! We'll continue after breakfast tomorrow." The king walked away, laughing about ants, leaving the two of them alone.

"Why did you do that?" Pavel asked. "No matter how tired I am, I'd still try for you."

"Oh, shush," answered the princess. "Now think. Both times you tried to hide, Father went into his study, came out and found you immediately. It was the same with Sasha and Misha, too."

"You think he has something in there to help him?" asked Pavel, impressed. "Lead the way!"

They crept through the corridors and into the king's study. Shelves covered the walls, holding old, leathery books and strange figures, instruments and ancient weapons. Beams of light squeezed through a large, grimy window, highlighting the dust in the air. In front of the window was a huge desk, and on it was a book, open to a blank page.

"It'll take hours to search all of this!" cried Pavel. "We might be in trouble."

"We've got time," answered Olga, looking around, "as long as Father doesn't walk in. I wonder where he is – "

The open book gave a sudden jump on the desk.
Lines started to appear on the empty paper, and then
a picture of the king in a huge bath with a beard made
of bubbles …

"I think I have a plan," said Pavel.

⚜ Chapter 7 ⚜

They met in the dining hall the next morning. The king hummed happily as he finished his last piece of toast. He rubbed his stomach, pleased with himself, and looked at the prince. "Well, are you ready, lad?" he asked, smiling.

"I need a miracle to equal your cunning," answered Pavel, winking at Olga. "But I'll try my best."

The king covered his face and began counting.

The princess quietly kissed Pavel on the cheek and smiled as she stepped back. He turned into a magpie, and the bird flew around Olga's head once, then out of a window.

"… two, one, zero! Ready or not, here I come!" cried
the king. "We must do this more often. What fun!"
He dashed straight to his study and closed the door.
Olga waited outside … and waited.

Finally, the door creaked, and the king poked his head out.

"Is there a problem, Father?" the princess
asked, innocently.

"Er … no," he said, scratching his head. "None at all.
I'll be back in a moment." He walked down the corridor,
slowly at first, then more and more quickly. He looked
in every room he passed.

Then he started opening drawers and cupboards.
He searched under sofas. He picked up cushions,
squeezed them, and threw them aside. He did the same
to a cat and quickly learnt not to squeeze cats.

He ran out into the palace grounds, tossed hay around in barns, shouted at horses and poked sticks into ant holes. Eventually, sweaty and dirty, he trudged back to his study. "I don't understand," he moaned. "The book always tells me where everyone is!"

Olga followed and patted his arm as they looked down at a blank page in the magical book. "There, there, Father," she said. "Have a closer look."

As he peered closer, the page broke away from its binding and grew. It became as big as a man and began to change shape. In an instant, Prince Pavel was standing on top of the desk, a huge grin on his face. He'd turned himself into a blank page in the magical book to fool the king …

Chapter 8

The king was grumpy about it, but he'd given his word. Olga and Pavel were going to be married. As they wrote hundreds of invitations, the king mumbled about being beaten by a boy. While they talked to a chef about the wedding banquet, he complained about stupid magic that didn't work properly. He even moaned during Olga's meeting with the dressmaker, this time about how expensive everything was going to be.

"Father's been sulking for days," said Olga later, walking in the gardens with Pavel. "I don't know what to do."

"I'm a little nervous about having an angry king as a father-in-law, too," answered Pavel. "If only he didn't have to be the best all the time – "

"That's it!" she cried. "Pavel, you're a genius!" She turned and ran back into the palace, leaving her husband-to-be standing amongst the flowers feeling very confused.

The king was in the dining hall poking at his porridge with a spoon, growling to himself about good-for-nothing princes, when Olga sprinted in.

"Father," she said, gasping for breath. "I know you're upset – "

"He's not good enough for you, that one," the king cried. "He's lucky! That's all, lucky!"

"Oh, Father! Just listen," she said. "Everyone knows you're the smartest, cleverest king ever."

"Go on," said the king.

"The only reason I like Pavel is that he's nearly as clever as you," she said, knowing what would cheer up the king. "And we've thought of the perfect wedding gift for you."

"What's that?" the king snapped. "The bill for your honeymoon?"

"There'll be hundreds of guests at the wedding," she grinned at him. "It'll be the perfect opportunity for tricks – tricks to prove just how clever you are."

The king's face froze for a second, and then lit up with the biggest smile his daughter had ever seen. He pulled her into a huge hug. "Oh, my girl! My brilliant girl!"

And everyone lived happily ever after.

Everyone except the wedding guests, that is ...

Hide-and-seek

I found you!

I found you too!

You can't hide from me ...

... however small you make yourself!

Oh, you win ...

... even if I am the cleverest king ever!

Ideas for reading

Written by Clare Dowdall, PhD
Lecturer and Primary Literacy Consultant

Reading objectives:
- increase familiarity with a wide range of books including fairy stories and retell orally
- identify themes and conventions in a wide range of books
- identify main ideas drawn from more than one paragraph and summarise ideas

Spoken language objectives:
- give well-structured descriptions, explanations and narratives for different purposes

Curriculum links: PSHE – health and well-being; Art – drawing

Resources: paper and pencils; ICT for research; digital camera

Build a context for reading
- Look carefully at the front cover together and ask children to describe what they can see.
- Discuss what a folk tale is, and what features might be found in folk tales.
- Read the blurb. Discuss what being clever means, and ask children to name a famous person who's clever. Think about how clever people might behave.

Understand and apply reading strategies
- Read pp2–3 with the children. Discuss what kind of person the king is.
- Ask children to read pp4–5 silently and to build up an idea of what the king is like, e.g. kind, silly, vain, funny, arrogant...
- Ask children to read on to find out who the cleverest character in the story is.